W9-BNG-089
BOOK SOLD
NO LONGER R.H.P.L.
PROPERTY

ADVENTURE TIME™

VOLUME 4

#1
BABE

kaboom!
TM

CN
CARTOON NETWORK.

FREDERATOR

A catalog record of this book is available from OCLC and from the KaBOOM! website, www.boom-studios.com, on the Librarians Page.

BOOM! Studios, 5670 Wilshire Boulevard, Suite 450, Los Ange g.
ISBN: 978-1-60886-351-8, eISBN: 978-1-61398-205-1

CREATED BY
Pendleton Ward

WRITTEN BY
Ryan North

ILLUSTRATED BY
Shelli Paroline & Braden Lamb

ADDITIONAL COLORS BY
Lisa Moore

LETTERS BY
Steve Wands

COVER BY
Drew Weing

ASSISTANT EDITOR
Whitney Leopard

EDITOR
Shannon Watters

TRADE DESIGN
Stephanie Gonzaga
& Hannah Nance Partlow

With special thanks to
Marisa Marionakis, Rick Blanco, Curtis Lelash, Laurie Halal-Ono, Keith Mack, Kelly Crews and the wonderful folks at Cartoon Network.

E-MART
STOP, MAGIC MAN! I WON'T LET YOU HURT THEM!
A little magic never hurt anyone...
...as long as that "anyone" is me! Hee hee!

FIVE MINUTES EARLIER:
Would you pass the tea, Ghost Princess 2?
Oh um it would be my pleasure, Princess Bubblegum! And please, call me "Spookette."
Spookette! What a perfectly excellent name!

I'm so glad the Princess Tea Party happened during summer this year. It's so hard to find a nice winter dress!
I made this hat out of a breakfast taquito!
It's delightful!

You asked me to make sure you didn't break your "no sammiches" diet!
Past Me was dumb to go on that diet! Past Me didn't remember how tasty sammiches are!

So I was all, **MELISSA**, don't even talk to me like you know my business, 'cause I know you don't know! And I know you know I know you don't know!
I don't know why she even says that junk! Save it for your dumb diary, you know?
Wow, how--um... interesting!
SQUEEZ-E-MART
Uh... yes?

Oh my glob, Hot Dog Princess, you'll love this: do you have **ANY IDEA** what the very next thing she said to me was?
Nope.
NOTHING!
She hung up her lumping phone on me!
She didn't even say "Oh wow, peace out **LSP**, you know I gotta go be jealous of your mad lumps now!" Can you even **BELIEVE HER?**
Wow.

I swear to glob, I love her, but I cannot lumpin' stand her sometimes. You know how it's like you're friends, but you kinda can't stand to be around them sometimes because they're **SO LUMPIN' ANNOYING??**
Uhh...
SQUEEZ-E-MART
I know just the feeling, ladies!

Everything's going so well! Should we warn the princesses about what we saw on the previous page? Naw, it's probably... it's probably fine. Right?

There's this one person who just won't stop talking and talking and talking and it makes me want to shut her up for good, you know? Like, with magic? Magic I can never take back?
Oh my glob, don't even get me started on chatty talk pals wh--
MAGIC MAN!

That's my name, don't wear it out! Because I don't think it'd look good on you anyway, Princess... Bubblegum, right? It really wouldn't go with your hair, sweetheart.
What do you want, Magic Man? Why don't you find some other tea party to crash?

Crash? Why Bubblegum, that sounds perfectly delightful. MAAAAAAGIC!
Hey, I know how you are with words and irony and junk! DON'T DO ANY DUMB IRONIES ON US!

Too late, Bubbles!
My tea! I DIDN'T GET TO LUMPIN' DRINK IT YET!
My sammiches!
My breakfast taquito!

Man, how come we're not allowed in? I like chatting up friends and I have fancy clothes I look nuts in! Scope these mad threads!
Broshanks you know that's not a suit you say no to, but rules is rules: princesses only.

That's the first rule of Princess High Tea! Plus the way you've been raising your tea-sippin' pinkie has been mad sloppy of late.
Dude I know I gotta buckle down and blast my pinkies.
My quads are PRETTY blasted, but I was thinkin' of blastin' up my ligamen--
ANCIENT PSYCHIC TANDEM WAR ELEPHANTS?!

Multiple Sets Of Ancient Psychic Tandem War Elephants, Plural?!

That was weird. I thought there was only one of those guys, and we set him free to explore the world and also his emotions!
Yeah, and it's almost like he came from the Princess High Tea...**OH DANGS!**

Dude, we gotta get there faster! Jake Suit me, bro?
Twice in one day?
It's fine! **MY QUADS ARE READY!**
JAAAAAAKE!
SUUUUUIT!
I guess this is the...**HOT** new look this season?
STOP IT WITH THE IRONIC MAGIC, YOU BUTT!
Guys! Nobody drink me in, okay?!

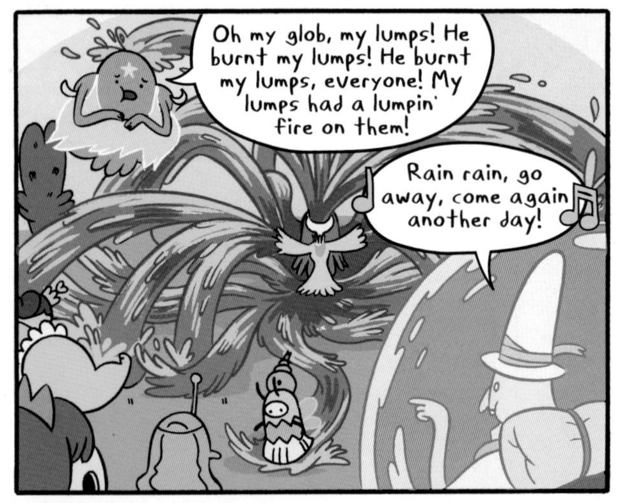
Oh my glob, my lumps! He burnt my lumps! He burnt my lumps, everyone! My lumps had a lumpin' fire on them!
Rain rain, go away, come again another day!

You guys, my lumps were on **LUMPIN' FIRE!** They'll never lump in quite the same way! I gotta call Melissa!
Oh my glob, your stupid voice! My magic now removes it: **NOICE**.
SQUEEZ-E-MART
Noooooooo--

--ooooooooo!
KSSSSHHHHT

LIFE HACK: Think "What would Magic Man do?" and then do the opposite in every single situation and you will be kind and well-loved forever.

Oh, hey guys, you wanted to crash this party too, huh? Well, I'm out. PEACE!
Jake!
FINN!

You...you saved me, Finn and Jake! Oh, I knew you'd put your life on the line for me someday, but I had no idea it would be so... so DRAMATIC!
I promise I won't forget this. I won't lumpin' forget this.

Guys? Oh my glob oh my glob oh my GLOB, if you guys croaked saving me I don't know what I'll do! It's almost too much drama to handle! Finn, speak to me! Jake, squeeze my hand ever so softly!
SQUEEZ-E-MART

They're okay!
AHHH, SO EPIC!

Well, that's another High Tea completely ruined. I swear, it's almost like gathering every princess together in an undefended forest glen invites jerks to come mess with us! Do you know where Magic Man might've gone to, Finn?
?
!!

What--
--what'd you just say?
Oh my glob, the spell was real! They saved me but at a terrible cost! MY HEROES LOST THEIR LUMPIN' VOICES!

I don't know why you're reading this down here when such nutty things are happening up above.
I don't know what's going to happen! I find out at the same time you do!

No, not--quite? They're still talking, but it's weird. Jake, say "yes"!
Interest-ing. Finn, where do you live?

You guys understood that, right? That thumbs up meant "yes"!
Looks like as long as Finn and Jake can represent what they want to say visually, they can say it. But it sounds so weird!
Oh my glob! Finn and Jake, I've never heard anyone say things like that before. It's so lumpin' beautiful!

This is beyond anything I've encountered before. I'm, uh, not sure how to cure you.
Will you lose your regular voices forever? I...

I don't know. This is dark nutty magic, boys.
But couldn't Magic Man turn them back?

That's exactly the problem: he's a total butt! I don't think he'd do it willingly.
Then we'll have to change his mind...with our fists! WE GOTTA GIVE HIM HIS LUMPS!
Well gosh, we can't attack directly 'cause he'll just magic us too! We need to prank the prankster somehow, you know? Force him to take his awful magic back!

I dunno how long this'll take, Jake.
Maybe you should go home and rest up? We'll send for you when we've got a plan.

Is there an award for making a picture of a cartoon butt into actual, important dialogue, because if so I want it.

I promise, we'll call for you when we need you.
No buts, Finn. We'll see you later, okay?
Don't worry you guys! We'll figure this out! We're gonna use our princess skills, okay?

Oh wow, are we doing emoticons?! BMO's the best at emoticons!

;)

BMO has been waiting since forever for a talking-in-emoticons competition! Years of extensive imaginary training is about to pay off!

MAY 6

×3!

???
:D

Sandwiches do not work that way BMO. I've tried. Oh how I've tried.

RIP

That stinky baby took a boom boom! Come on, stinky baby. What are you even doing?

#1

!
=???

-N+E+ !
ADVENTURE TIME!

Oops, was that cheating? Oh no!
Oops, is this also cheating? OH NO!

That's no pot! That's an *URN*.

BRRRRRING!
BMO

Okay guys, we've got a plan to take down Magic Man. Can you meet us back at High Tea?
Cool beans. Bubblegum out!

Glad you could make it, guys. We're ready to move against Magic Man, but we need to know where his base is. Can you tell us?

Wow. You know, there may actually be some upsides to talking like this.
I can't hear it! Speak up already, Finn!

Okay, I can hear it now.

In the script I said this scene included "Battle Damaged Action Hero Princesses" and I can honestly not think of a better combination of any five words than those.

Okay, so here's the plan: every princess will use her skillset to lay a separate trap outside Magic Man's house, all to be sprung simultaneously. For example, mine will be science-themed.
Mine will be a pit full of water!
Mine will be a mouth full of awful lampreys!

Then we knock on his door! When he comes out he's gonna get covered in a big ol' lumpload of traps!
Then you demand he give you your voice back, and if he doesn't, we'll just k
I can hear you, you know!
SQUEEZ-E-MART

What kind of plan was it to discuss the plan outside my house? I'm magic, man! And I'm keeping Finn and Jake's voices forever now!
I'm gonna sell them to jerks so they can make prank phone calls with 'em!
Finn and Jake will get in trouble because people will think it was them!

We won't let that happen, guys, I promise. We'll come up with a new plan, and this time we **WON'T** discuss it in earshot of the bad guy. By the way, thanks for the **REAL GREAT IDEA** you had, Let's All Discuss Our Plans In Front Of The Bad Guy Princess!
I'm sorry!
Also my name's Samantha

Oh my glob you guys I think I've got it! I seriously think I've got it!
Everyone let's go away from this jerk so I can tell you my lumpin' plan in private!
?

Okay! Don't come back ever, okay? Stay away now!

Yes hello my name is Samantha and I do not appreciate being the victim of most sarcasms

JOIKS MONTHLY

Hey, Magic Man! We came back!
And we brought some FRIENDS!
JOIKS MONTHLY

Our friends are these kick-butt weapons and junk, yah goon!
Give Finn and Jake back their voices right now, Magic Man, or I might just get tired of telling my friends here not to blow you up.

You just don't get it! You brought guns to a magic fight, ladies. Here, have a spell! It turns whatev's in your hands into stinky snakes!
Have fun with it!

What? How--?
WHAT THE BARFS ARE YOU DOING?

I take it back. "Super Awesome Armored Battle Princesses" is a pretty good five-word combination too.

Ha! That's for me to know and for you to obsess about for years until it eats you up inside, you butt!

Now do I start pulling triggers here and seeing what happens?
You wouldn't dare--
What the--?!

Wildberry Princess, why not give him a taste of your Wildberry Punch?
My pleasure.

Weeeee!

Okay fine, fine, have your dumb voices back! I spent a lot of time making this house just the way I like it, and I don't like it with holes in the dang roof!
BRAM

Y'all don't have my stentorian tones anyway.

Y'all be mad nasally

My voice, she's back!
Mine too! It's all I remembered and more!

Thank you, Magic Man. I hope you've learned a lesson here, and that lesson is don't be a jerk, or at the very least don't be a jerk to strangers for no reason.
Actually, all I've learned is how you tricked me, and now I've got a brand new way to mess with chumps in the future! Thaaaaaank youuuu!
Jake, check this noise my voice can make! Whooby whooby whoo
Nice, but check this! Bloopa bloopa poopa scoopa

Come on everybody, let's go back to Bubblegum's place for some popcorn and free snacks! We can leave this meany alone with his meany feelings!
Later, skater!

Thanks for helping us out, Princesses!
Yeah, we couldn't have done it without you!
Oh my glob, same to you! We made SUCH a great team. I guess we're all each other's heroes now, huh?
Skateboard Princess lives for this!

You know what? You never miss speaking until you can't do it, at least in the same phonological way.
I hear you, buddy.
THE END.

LATE THAT EVENING:
Busy day, huh Finn?
The busiest! But we rocked it.

Yeah we did. I bet we're gonna rock tomorrow's face too. Goodnight, bro!
Goodnight!

Hey, Finn?
Yeah Jake?
I ♥ you too, buddy

BUMP!

Hey, Ice King! You wanna see what THIS button does?
In a sec!
I'm gonna show you what THIS button does first!
You guys, stop figuring out the controls and lumpin' SAVE ME ALREADY!!
Here, have some ICE-SEEKLES!
This cage is lumpin' COLD! It's AWFUL in here, Finn!!
They're heat-seeking missiles made of ice, so I thought, "Ice King, you know what you should call these?" Then I thought, "No, what?"
And THEN I thought "ICE-SEEKLES!" I don't mind telling you, it was a great day for ol' Ice King.
OH MY GLOB!
NOBODY CARES!

— Next time, let's do it the other way, and I'll shrink down and climb inside **YOUR** head to operate the controls!

What could possibly go wrong?? —

"Finally," I thought, "Finally, things are going to go my way. This is just the beginning. It's gonna be 100% different for me from now on."

BOOM
LUMPIN' FINALLY.

You okay, LSP?
Uh, I'm fabulous, Finn! I'm always fabulous, and you should know that about me by now! HONESTLY.

But I lumpin' want out now, okay?
Okay okay, just a sec! We had to beat up Ice King first.
Did you see? We had cool suits!!

I dunno why I chose her anyway. She's, like, my #1 least favorite princess by far.
"Least"?! THAT'S a super dumb way to pronounce "BEST ALL-TIME ULTIMATE FOREVER"!!

It's like--way off from how it's normally pronounced. Not even close, Ice King. You really dropped the ball on this one. I gotta say.

A'yoop!
CRASH
Thanks guys. I don't wanna make things too **REAL** or junk, but I guess you're basically my heroes now, huh? You're **KINDA** true ultimate heroes.

TRUE ULTIMATE HEROES

TRUE ULTIMATE HEROES

KA-CHAK!
Whoa!
What the--?

Oh my glob! Are you guys alright?!
I think so! I landed on my butt. It's nicely padded!!
Mine too!

Wait, how come you fell down? Couldn't you have hovered in the air like LSP?
What?! I thought you guys wanted me to come along! You know: pals on an adventure, facing adversity, being drawn closer together because of it...
Pals!

• This trap door was locked with lock words. Which is perfect, because it means you need a key word to unlock it.

Whoa! I think I remember this place! I think--I think I **BUILT** this place.
These sound like fake words, Ice King! These sound like imaginary untruths you're dropping on us!
You really built this?

Yeah, I did! Years and years ago. Me and a couple of the guys, we had this **CRAAAZEE** plan.
Wait, which guys?
I dunno. It was years ago! But I do remember me and Hunson talking about--
Hunson? **HUNSON ABADEER??**
Listen, you wanna hear the story or not?
Yes please.
Good. Thank you, Jake.

"Anywho, like I said, I don't remember most of it, but I'm **PRETTY SURE** we had this big ol' master plan.
"There were machinations, you know?
"I remember we had some good times figuring out the machinations.
"Hmmm..."

Yeah, now I remember! This is a dungeon built specifically to test any heroes that enter it! It's **TRUE ULTIMATE HEROES ONLY**. Ooh, and there's prizes at the end!
Heroes?!
PRIZES?!

NIIIIIIICE

Heroes?! *PRIZES?!* And you're *CERTAIN* these are together at last in one non-stop thrill ride??

So you guys wanna go through this dungeon with me?
WITH you? I thought you said it was ultimate heroes only!
Well I mean normally it's heroes only, but I'm sure there'd be no trouble with you two tagging along with me.

Wait. Ice King, you...think you're a hero?
Ha ha! Right, because I'm TOTALLY the bad guy. Good one, Finn! You're a funny guy, you know that?
YOU KIDNAP PRINCESSES!!

Are you kidding, Jake? I don't KIDNAP princesses, guys! I rescue 'em.
From what?
Ha!
...You're serious?

"The lot in life of a princess is a sad one, guys. She's destined from birth to be trapped in the boring, tedious role of a head of state. Believe me, I know how it is!

"Oh, the endless meetings! The infinite series of petty disputes all needing YOUR personal intervention! Those dang flippin' spurns that patient merit of the unworthy takes!

"But don't princesses DESERVE only the best things in life? What if--like YOU, Jake--she wants excitement? What if--like YOU, Finn--she wants adventure?
"What if, like me, she even wants... COMPANIONSHIP??

"I rescue princesses from boredom, guys! From loneliness! I rescue them from not having ME in their lives!"
Save me, Ice King!! Also I lumpin' love you or whatever!

In the script these panels are described as "Ice King-O-Vision." Which is also the name of a brand of ice glasses I'd wear in a heartbeat.

But then you guys appear and usually mess everything up, but it's fine. I know we're pals, you guys just don't know any better.
S'cool.
Wow, you know, I never looked at it that way befor--
What about that time you made a monster wife out of stolen stitched-together princess body parts?!
"Oh, her? The woman who you made feel SO BAD that, one night, she left...forever?!"
Finn, this conversation isn't as fun as usual. It's SAD!
It's buzzing up my mind juices!
Anyway, ancient history! Forget the whole deal. So you guys wanna explore this dungeon or WHAT?
Just a couple of pals in the bowels of the earth, am I right?

It's buzzing up my mind juices! I'm serious, dude! I've updated my mind juice status to "buzzed up"!!

Come on, it'll be fun! Let's go do some dungeon activities together!
Jake, I **WAS** kinda born for this. I was kinda **LITERALLY BORN** to explore dungeons.
I was literally born on account of other, more biological reasons!!

Ice King, we consent to exploring this dungeon with you!!
Yeah mans!
HOORAY!!

Okay, so don't think about me or whatever! Just ignore me for a whole conversation like it's no big deal!

WhatEVER! I didn't wanna go into some gross old dungeon anyway!! I got plans, guys! I got DATES to go on!
I GOT HOTTIES LINED UP TO SMOOCH ON THESE LUMPS, AND NONE OF THEM LIVE IN HOLES!!

ONLY A FEW OF THEM LIVE IN HOLES!!

THEY DECORATED THEM REAL NICE. YOU DON'T EVEN KNOW.

DUNGEON I AM GOING TO GO BEAT UP THE BAD GUYS INSIDE YOU NOW!!
DUNGEON I AM GOING TO DO THE SAME, I'M PRETTY SURE!!
Yay, activities with friends!

Dang it, it's way dark here. You guys got anything for this? All I got is cold magic all up ons.
A hero never arrives unprepared!

It's true! I tell him, "Finn, brotimes, I don't think we're gonna need like a whole pack of pens on this adventure," and you know what he says?
"Let's invite Ice King right away, he's lots of fun and I like him"?
No, he says "You never know!"
Close, though.

Torches, what what!
Try using these when you want to look at things in darkened areas!

Thanks Finn.
Why do you think I wear a backpack all the time? Can't hold it all in my hands!

...WHOA.
Dude, you built... a HALL OF JUSTICE?!

HALL OF ★ JUST ICE
No man, check the kerning. It's a Hall of **JUST ICE!** I made it myself!
Out of ice, basically!

Ice and congealed feelings, yep yep!

What are we waiting for?
Nothing! Who said we were waiting? We're not waiting for anything! I'm not waiting!

CREEEAAAK
PFFFSSH!

GAH!

Oh yeah, I remember this piece! I called this snow sculpture "Why Oh Why Do I Have Problems Interacting With Women, Is It Because There's Something Broken With Me??"
PFFFFFT

I was going through some stuff, okay?

Third in my very successful "Reading The Title Of This Piece Will Make You Uncomfortable" series

Hey, this looks like a pretty sweet dungeon, Ice King!
Thanks!
And you're sure you don't remember what sort of monsters you put in here?
Nope!
I bet they're nutty ice-themed. Like, ice skeletons! Ice teeth-beasts!
We could beat them with fire!
See anything down there, Jake?
Nothing yet!
Oh wait, nevermind. They're just regular ol' icicles!
PHEW
...you know, if we actually had any.
Guys! I think I see a giant teethbeast ahead!!
You guys go ahead and scope it out for your ol' friend Ice King, okay?
Wait, I think I heard something up ahead! I'ma check it out!
Polynomial!!
Hey, how did you keep everything from melting down here?
Magic?
I guess??
Nope. No monsters here after all!
ICE-Y what you mean!
Heard 'em all before, guys.

Who dares disturb the icy slumber of the **THREE EYEBABES??**
Whoa!
I'm Jake the dog and he's Finn the human!
And **I'M** Ice King and I'm pretty sure I created you three fine ladies, so step to the side please. Pappa's coming through.

Man, y'all sound like chumps! Attack!!
LEVEL TWO ICEY STARE!
LEVEL THREE ICEY STARE!!

Level **THREE?** When'd you learn level three?
Last week! I looted a magazine. You was nappin'.
Attack harder, please!!

Jake, you distract them while I sneak up behind them and slice 'em in two!
Got it!
I'm a critical part of this team!

Um, surprise! Hello, female monsters, I am a male monster designed to be distractingly hot to you! Here I am! Wooby wooby woo!
That's patronizing and stupid!
Attack him harder!!

No really! I'm honestly a hunky man who wants to get dates done with you!
I'd rather date a rat with, like, spider-legs!!
Whoa. Really? Okay, no, I can do that!

Bleh
For justice!!
Bleh
I for one am just glad I don't have to talk to that guy anymore.

One thing you need to know about eye monsters is that they have interests beyond dating strangers they just met in a cave.

Hey those were pretty great monsters, huh guys?
Yeah, not bad! I liked the part where we defeated 'em.
Look, they left something behind!
It's a note! It has a picture of a duck on it! Weird.
A duck?
Oh I get it! We were supposed to duck!
Ouch!
Who dares destroy my three Eyebabes: the Triptych Herald of me...
Ouch!!
...The ICE QUEEN?!
Whoa!
Dude, you made a lady version of yourself as an enemy?! What's going on in your head, man? Why you gotta make things weird??
I don't know, I don't know! It just happens so easy!
Um, hey there Ice Queen? I'm Ice King, and I'm the one who made you--
--this whole dungeon actually, I was going through some stuff with my relationships and...
...ANYWAY I'm here to get the treasure I left behind here and then forgot about? When I built this dungeon?
...and also you?
Ice King? Is it really you? My gosh, I haven't looked on your face for--how long has it been? Two hundred years?
Sure, maybe! Who's counting, right?
Yep, it's been two hundred years since you snuck out saying you were "gonna check out what's...over there" and NEVER CAME BACK.
Man I really gotta find a better way to work through my feeliiiiiiiings

Well, maybe THIS is a better way to do it!!

Why are you mad at me, baby? What's inside your heart?
You want I should check?
Hey hey hey!
BZZZZZ

KATHOOM
Whoa!
Why? Why would you create me only to do this?
Jake, do you think it's weird that all the enemies in Ice King's dungeon are ladies?
Finn, that is the least of the things here I'm currently uncomfortable with.
Thanks for rescuing me, guys! Ice King trapped me inside her long ago to power her secondary regality processor. It's been a difficult couple of centuries!
Which way's out?
Just go that way.
You'll know you're in the right direction if you're moving away from the interesting stuff, like fun fights with ice monsters and stuff!
Thanks! Goodbye forever!!

Rock Candy Lady gets home and discovers the bad news is that while she was frozen all her kids got old, but the good news is they also got AWESOME. Seniors on skateboards, etc. She's totally down with this.

SOON:
You seemed surprised Ice Queen was down here, man. You really don't remember much about this place, do you?
Finn, when you get older you'll realize some things, and one of those things is that memories blow so hard sometimes.

Huh?
You know, like leaves? Like how memories can blow out of your head like leaves off a tree and you end up forgetting things?
Memories! They can blow so hard!!

I can't remember everything for a thousand years, Finn. There's only so much room up here! Every new memory I make pushes out an old one, and a lot of those old ones are things nobody else remembers anymore.
These dang ol' memories are precious, Finn, or at least I thought they were before I forgot the reasons why. There's stuff up here that I--

--that I don't want to lose.

DUDE, STOP MAKING ME SAD!

WHY ARE YOU SO GOOD AT THIS PARTICULAR SKILL, ICE KING?!

Why don't you just write 'em down?
You don't think I didn't try that? I got rooms full of books, and each book's full of things that I don't understand why I wrote 'em down in the first place!
I try reading 'em sometimes--but either I forget what I read, or I remember what I read and I forget what I wanted to remember!

Thhppptth.

Anyway, whatever! I don't wanna bring you guys down. We're a couple of heroes on a journey into darkness, huh? That's us: a couple of pals looking for a fun time in a dark cold place!!

Look, a clear patch in the ice! Maybe there's treasure down there, right?

...I don't see anything.
Well, come on, look harder! There's got to be some treasure here somewhere!
If the treasure ends up being the water we're looking into I'm gonna be cheesed, guys!
Water's like the freest thing ever!

It **LITERALLY FALLS FROM THE SKY**, Finn!!
I hear you, dude!

You can often find it on the ground, collected into tremendous puddles I call "lakes"!

Alright, well, there's gotta be some treasure here somewhere...
Come on, Finn!
Wait, I...
...I think I see something moving??
AAAAAAAA
AAAAAA
OMG! Treasure!

I'm serious, I think I saw something move!
I wanna see!

You can't see anything through this dang ice! Here.

Ha! See? What's the matter? Impressed I can CONTROL ICE ITSELF with my MAGICAL POWERS??
SSSSK
No that's like your whole deal! It's right there in your name, dude.
We've seen you do it like infinity times.
CRACK

Better?
Hmm.

TAP
TAP
Yeah, I guess it definitely was nothing after all. Oh well!!

It's okay, Ice King. *I'M* impressed you can control ice. All I can control is air, and then only if it's in my lungs, and then only if I blow it out on someone.

WHOA!!!
Whoa!
Whoa!!
FISHO THE COLOSSAL
ICE DUNGEON BOSS
She--she grew into the name over time.

Finn! How you wanna play this?
I dunno. Rubber buns?
THAT, my friend, is DISCRETE MATH.

BWOOMP

HOW DID PEOPLE EVEN FIGHT BEFORE WE INVENTED THE RUBBER BUN MANEUVER?
NO IDEA, DUDE!!

Hey Fishface! You're on the menu, and today's special is...um...
SUSHI!!
Yeah! Sushi!

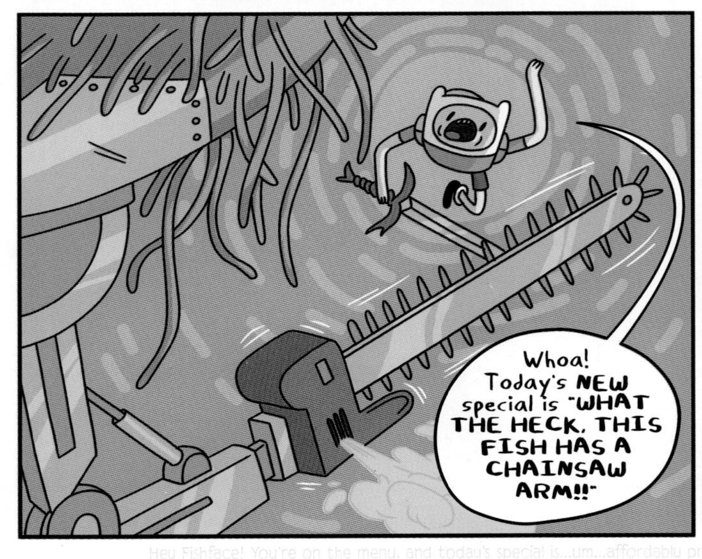

Whoa! Today's NEW special is "WHAT THE HECK, THIS FISH HAS A CHAINSAW ARM!!"

What are you, new?

Hey Fishface! You're on the menu, and today's special is...um...affordably priced and sure to please the whole family?!

Hey, thanks for saving my buns, Ice King!
S'cool!

Easy peasy lemon squeezy!

GLOOSH
Aw man!!
I forgot how the insides of bodies are 100% gross 100% of the time!

Karate chop! Hi-yah!
Good work, Ice King!
S'yeah!

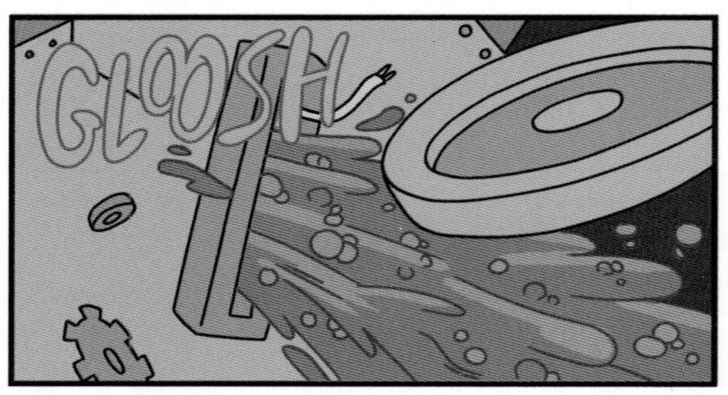
GLOOSH

Aw man, twice in one day?!
Your horoscope was right, dude!!

FINN: you will get covered in gross guts twice in one day. So, um, try to act surprised?

JAKE: an unexpected revelation unlocks an ancient secret which has the power to destroy the planet. DON'T MESS THIS UP, DUDE.

LEMONGRAB: Okay sir--SIR, please, if you'll just--SIR. SIR, you need to CALM DOWN.

BLEHHHH
KABOOM!

Jake, browich, you didn't really help much there!
You guys had it handled! I figured I'd sit this one out and work through some personal stuff instead, you know?

Real talk: mad stuff got worked through, Finn. Personal revelations got figured out like NUTS.
Big ups to that!
KAPOW!!
Gah!
BUMP!

Hey neat, the way out!
That's not the way out! We're not even halfway done yet!
That fish must've just, I don't know, eaten some explosions earlier or something!!

Listen I don't know how bodies work, but that seems to be the most likely explanation.
OKAY WHATEVER WHO CARES LET'S GO CLAIM OUR DUNGEON TREASURE!!

oh no that trip to the explosion buffet isn't sitting too well

Well, if it's anywhere it's down there. Water bosses **ALWAYS** hide their treasure in the water. That's the first rule of water bosses!
ONE PROBLEM: both of us are incredibly awful at breathing water. Like, we're so bad at breathing water that if we tried it we'd **DIE**.

Hmm...I've got an idea. Jake, can you stretch your nose and mouth away from your face?
You mean like...

...**THIS??**
You guys got a plan or what?
Does **THIS** answer your question, Ice King??

Hold on, I said that too soon. This obviously doesn't answer your question.
One sec.

SOON:
Okay, now it works.
Does **THIS** answer your question, Ice King??

Ladies and gentlemen, I give you: THE JAKEYSPHERE.

So, you guys do this...a lot?
Naw man. It's a sometimes treat.

This is it, man! This is the treasure!
I can't wait to see what I left behind here and then completely forgot about!

I've got something! I'm pulling it out!
Ahhh **SO EXCITING**

do do do de. do do do de. DO DO DO DE. DO DO DO DE DO DO DO DE DO DO DO DE....dah dah dah DAAAAH

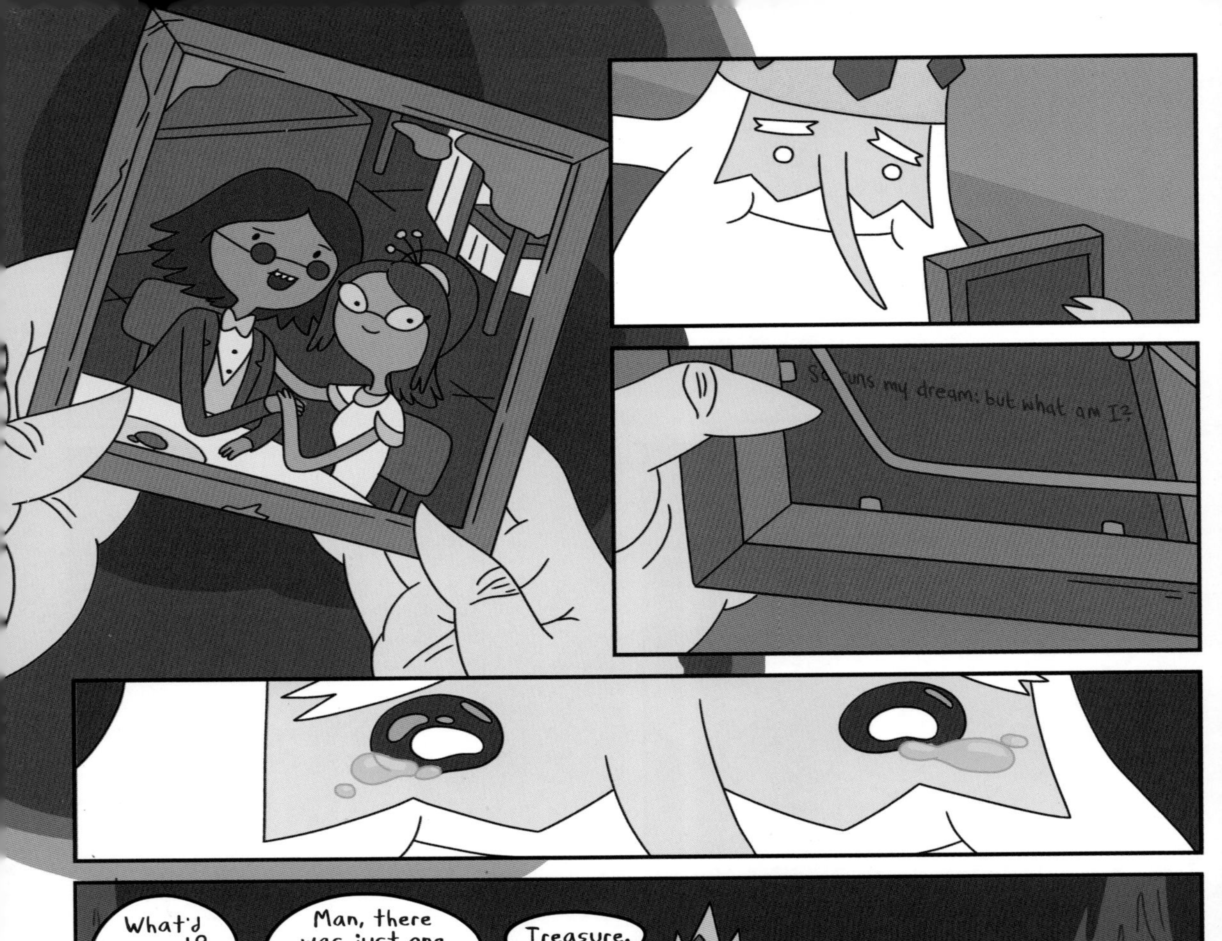
So runs my dream: but what am I?

What'd we get? What was inside?
Man, there was just one thing in it after all. It was--
Treasure.

It was the kind of treasure you don't take with you, Jake. You leave it there so you know you can always come back to it.
I don't understand! Explain it to me in great detail!

SHORTLY:
Now I understand but feel weird and sad!
WHAT A WORLD!!

Worlds, am I right??

SOON:
Well, that's it for my dungeon. The next one should be coming up soon though.
The one by Hunson Abadeer?!
Oh man oh man! Marceline's dad, the Lord of Evil, **AND** the ruler of the Nightosphere! This is gonna be tiiii-yiiiiight!!

Ha ha, it sure will! It will be quite bodacious! It'll be so ti-yight that you'll really wish it was looser! Math math math!
It--it's weird when you try to use our slang, Ice King.
Is that **REALLY** what we sound like?

Kinda, who knows? Anyway, here we are!
Welcome, gentlemen. Welcome to...

THE NIGHTOSPHERE'S NIGHTMAREOSPHERE
ACTUALLY A TOROID
Well, actually, you can read the sign as well as I can!
say fellows, how bodacious are you willing to get? Because I dare say at present I am willing to get quite bodacious indeed and I shan't hesitate to solicit like-minded company!

Odd. Normally skulls aren't so warm to the touch!

Peppermint Butler?!

HISSSSSS

HISSSSSS

HISSSSSS
Ha! That guy. It's always something with him, am I right?
Classic Pep-Butts!

Oh Peppermint Butler, we bump into you in the zaniest and most terrifying places!

What was he writing, dude?
Um..."The stars shall align, their cold and ancient light touching upon the ashes of His portrait and awakening the maddening horror"?

Whoa! He must've been writing a story!
Lucky for him I'M a professional author-type writing guy!!
We have to finish it for him!

LATER:
There! Much better.
Once upon a time
THE STARS ~~SHALL ALIGN~~ aligned, THEIR COLD AND ANCIENT LIGHT TOUCHING UPON THE ASHES OF HIS PORTRAIT AND AWAKENING THE MADDENING HORROR
of the awesome dudes, Finn and Jake!! They're rad at fights and love fun! They're in a spooky dungeon right now, WHOAH!!
Ice King is in this story too! Only here, his muscles are EVEN NICER. They're like, hold up, baby, where'd you get those dang pecs??
How many awards do you think we'll get?
All of them, I'm pretty sure?

I dunno! It's a great idea!

ACTIVITIES!!

This is a pretty great dungeon so far. How come your one didn't have a writing activity center, Ice King?

And it's nice how those crawlies open up to let us through, and then close up behind us!

I DUNNO, IT WAS MY FIRST DUNGEON

Yes, it's quite considerate! Ice King, how come your dungeon didn't have considerate crawlies?

And look at this bad guy all covered in gonk and junk! That's super intense!

Come on guys, you're making me feel bad about my dungeon choices. I'm learning with you!

Look at this! He's straight up attacking us! No chatting us up first or nothing!

This is a right proper dungeon.

CHKK CHHHHK

Oh right, too warm for my mad ice skills. Okay, whatever! He's all yours!

Leave him to me, friends!!

PFFFSSST

CHKK CHHHHK

CHKK CHHHHK

CHKK CHHHHK

Alley oop!

Man, the prize at the end of this dungeon is going to be **INTENSE**.

Obvs!!

EVERYONE'S FIRST DUNGEON IS A LEARNING EXPERIENCE. COME ON GUYS, I THOUGHT THIS WAS UNDERSTOOD

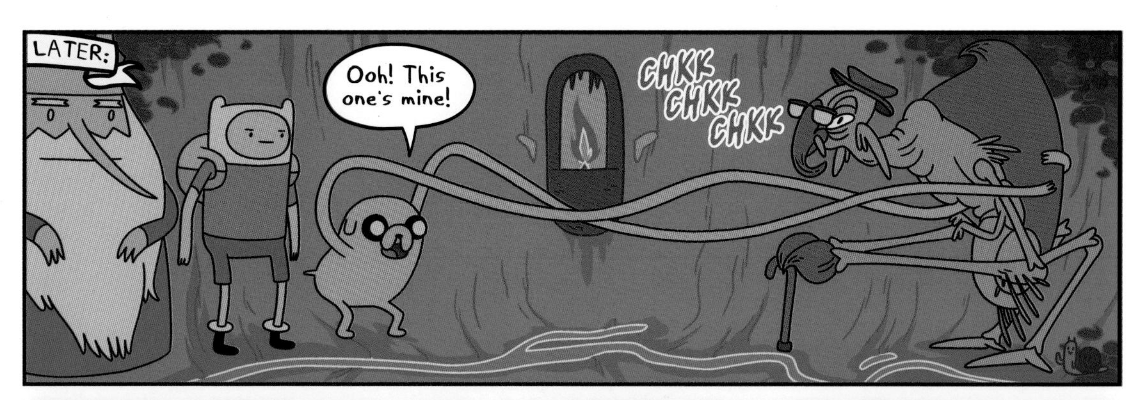
LATER:
Ooh! This one's mine!
CHKK CHKK CHKK

A'yup!
CHKK

LATER:
This one's just a baby! A wee baby monster!
CHKK CHHHHK
Okay, off you go into the gross pile of bugs, baby!!

LATER:
CHKK
CHKK
Hey, does this seem a little, like, easy to you guys?
I dunno, man. I feel like we're earning it, you know?

Ha ha, okay! This is fun! We're having fun!
Hey, is that a giant fist coming out of the wall?

POW!
Ow, front and center in my face! Right where I do all my smoochin'!!

Welcome to this all-expense tour of my lips. That's right, take a good look. Food goes in and smooches come out, baby.

Glob. What hit us?

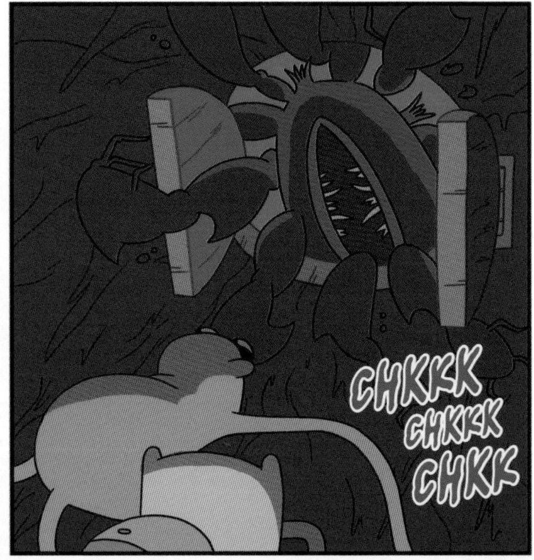
CHKKK
CHKKK
CHKK

CHKKK CHKK
HOOK CROOK
(GROSS-NASTY MODE)
ANCIENT UNKNOWABLE EVIL
Don't worry, guys, we got this! We'll beat this boss like an egg in a lemon meringue pie, which means he'll get whipped a heck of a--

CHHK
OOF!
--lot?

SMACK!
Blehhh

ICE KING!

OOOF!
CHKK CHHHHK
JAKE!!

Jake! Help me out here!!

JAKE!
Blehhh

Alright mister, you've knocked out my best friend. You've knocked out the weird old man I hang out with. And now you've made me MAD.
CHHKH CHKCCK CHKKKK

There's just one thing to do. Mister, I am going to--

CONTINUED NEXT CHAPTER

Oh wow, sorry, we got cut off there! Well, what was supposed to happen in panel six was--*SECRET TEXT ALSO CONTINUED NEXT CHAPTER*

Behold, we know not anything;
I can but trust that good shall fall
At last—far off—at last, to all
And every winter change to spring.
So runs my dream; but what am I?

And with no language but a cry.

CHKK
CHHHHK
Alright mister, you've knocked out my best friend. You've knocked out the weird old man I hang out with. And now you've made me **MAD**.

There's just one thing to do. Mister, I am going to--

cough

Haha whoa, I'm choking on my own saliva over here. Bleh.
Anyway.

MISTER, I'M GONNA GIVE YOU THE BIZ!!

Last chapter I was polite enough to cut away from Finn being all gross with his own mouth juices, but I've had a month to reconsider and in that time I have concluded YES INDEED, FULL GRAPHIC DETAIL IS WARRANTED

Take that!

CHKK CHHHHK
...Huh? Nasty!
SSSLLOP

Not allowed! I'm just gonna keep slicing!!

AAAAAAAAAAHHHGGGGGHH!

huff huff
SSSLLOP

Aw snap, a self-repairing monster! What is even the DEAL here?
DING

Don't judge! The Hook Crook's body is just doing what your body does, only faster. And grosser. And without bandages covering that nasty stuff up.

Aw snap, trying to attack me to death too? What is even the deal here AGAIN?!
CHKK

CHKK
CHHHHK
Aw snap, chasing me while you try to smush me to death?
WHAT IS EVEN THE DEAL HERE, I might add?!

CHKK
JAKE!

ICE KING!
CHKK
CHHHHK

CHKK
CHHHHK
WAKE UP, YOU GUYS!!

Hey it's me, Jake! I'm totally awake now! Woooo! Yep, Jake: that's definitely me!

Darn it, that's not good enough!!

I had such high hopes for it too!

CRACKLE
Hey, I'm the Ice King! Ice magic comes out of my body! I--

KAZZZT
Parametric!

Almost...
Almost...

Now!

KAZZZT
KAZZZT
KAZZZT

The magic was within him all along, and now it's COMING OUT.

YES!
Totally worth the weird after-taste!!

Whaa--?!

Hey, you guys beating up on ol' Ice King? My head feels like someone's punched it for realsies, and my bellyguts feel all stretched!
Finn?

Finn, are you--
Oh ha ha, I guess you didn't hear me come in...

Ice King! Duck!!
Okay!

...huh? Guys, what's going--

PTOOIE

LEVEL UP!
Oh wow! I LOVE WAKING UP LIKE THIS!

It's way better than waking up sad! Most things are!!

Hey. You did good back there, bro.
Thanks!
What gave you the idea to fill us up with air?

Huh.

Hey, check it out! There was treasure in the middle of that monster!
Dude! That's gotta be HUNSON ABADEER'S TREASURE!!

I TOTALLY CAN'T WAIT TO SEE WHAT'S INSIDE HERE, YOU GUYS.

Turn the page I wanna see too! Turn the page turn the page TURN THE PAGE

OH MY GLOB
I'M GETTING PRETTY TIRED OF THESE SUCKY TREASURES

KRAAAAAK
Whoa!
Is this--the way out?
Naw man, it looks more like an entrance? To, like, a skull land? Skullburg, maybe?

Ice King, you big silly! How could you forget the final dungeon?! SHEESH, you ol' goose.

There's one more dungeon? Hunson made another one?
No no, this was done by someone else.
You, uh, you threw him into the sun.

This, my friends, is the entrance to...
LICH LAND!

Skull Land? Skullburg? Skulltopia? Skull City? Skulltropolis? Metroposkull? Am I getting warmer?

That sounds amazing, y'all!
What! It's **INSANELY DEADLY**.

I mean, I've never been inside it, but I know I don't wanna mess around in there. You know how he built it?
No, how?
I have no idea, dogg!!

"He just appeared before me and Hunson during one of our dungeon meetings.
"That's the last thing we could remember.

"The next thing we knew it was three weeks later and we were starving. We lost three weeks.
"Hunson suspected he'd done something with our dungeons but didn't really care, and I never went down to check. After a while I forgot about it too.

We **HAVE** to go in there! We have a **HEROIC DUTY** to clean it out and to remove the Lich's evil influence!
The Lich hates everything, Finn! He's not cool like me! We go in there and we're definitely pooched!!

Um, no offense.
S'cool.

Some of my best friends are dogs

Ice King, I'm going in there and I'm going to kill any bad guys I find.
Yeah. If there's even a CHANCE he could come back, we have to go in there. We need to make sure he can't.
Guys!!

Ice King, you said you were a hero. Now's your chance to prove it.
Guys, can we PLEASE operate by unanimous consensus here? I really think--
I'm going in too!

I got your back.
Homies help homies, yo.

DARN IT YOU GUYS YOU KNOW I DON'T LIKE BEING PEER PRESSURED

DARN IT
AHHHHHHHH

SOMETIMES I THINK I NEED TO GET SOME BETTER PEERS. YOU KNOW, KINDA CLASS UP THAT WHOLE PEER AREA.

Whoa! What is this place?
Ruff!

Hold up, you can only talk in barks now? Dang man.
I feel different too: my face feels pointy and my arm got awesome. You wanna turn around and head back to where things are normal?

That's the spirit, buddy! Let's explore this weird farm world first. And if we find any evidence of the Lich, we destroy it! **WHAT TIME IS IT?!**
Baaark bark bark bark!
Yeah! It totally is that time right now!!

Aw man, this isn't a sword! I can't stab no fools with this ol' thing!
SNIFF SNIFF

Bro, wait up! We're on teams, remember?!
Hey, does your sense of smell feel stronger too?
SNIFF SNIFF

Does my sense of smell feel stronger? WHO NOSE?!

What are you on the trail of, Jake? Is it evil? Is it the--

--THE LICH?!

Wow, we're way math here! Already we've found the remnant of the Lich, and now there's nothing to do but crush it and rid this peaceful land of this evil influence forever!

Jake! We got a prize!

AND IT'S AMAZING!!

That's what I like to see! No wait, t-hats what I like to see. No wait, th-HATS what I like to see. Anyway you get the idea.

ELSEWHERE...
Whoa, dude. It brought us back home?
That's convenient!
Jake and Finn! BMO made lunch! It's cookies and cow milk, and the milk is straight from the inside of a cow!!
Dang, I love all those things!!
BMO

Huh? How come I can't stretch to get my snacktime treats?!
I dunno, dude! Normally you just go like this!

WHAAAAAAAAT?

Ha ha this is gonna be so much fun! You're gonna love having my powers, dude! They're great for everything!
You're not worried?

Naw man, we can always go back through the door and switch back. But while we're here in CRAZYLAND, let's have some fun! Hey, you think you can find any evidence of the Lich?

I'm on it, dude!! I'm gonna find Lich evidence like crazy. Check it!

You know, this is way easier than running around all over the place.
Heh. Yeah, it's--it's kinda the best.
BMO

Wait, I found something! It's like--the Lich's spine and hip, I think? It's at the bottom of a swamp. Hold on, I'm gonna bring it back and we can destroy it!
No need, dude! Just stretch yourself around it, crush it into powder, and then throw the powder into a fire or whatever. Or space. I dunno. Whatever's easiest.
Oh, right. Of course. It seems obvious now that you say it.
You'll get used to it! I tell you, my first few stretches were pretty amateur hour stuff too.
Hey Jake! Hey Finn!
Okay, I did that thing! NICE. The Lich's presence on this world has been destroyed!
Yay! Adventures!
That's great! Especially since I made this cake happen, and now we've got the perfect reason to eat it!

Looks delicious, PBubs! What kind of cake we dealing with here?
Dog treat cake! I tried some a few days ago, and guys, dog treats are mad tasty. I mean, they're meat flavored so in retrospect I guess it was KINDA obvious.
NICE.

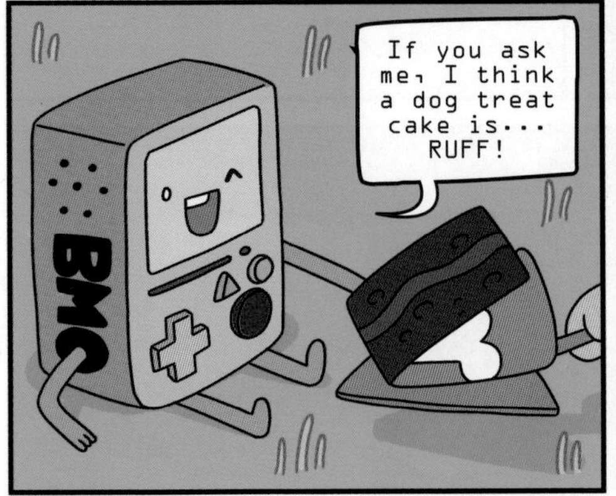
If you ask me, I think a dog treat cake is... RUFF!
BMO

BMO THE BAD PUNS ARE DOWN HERE, WHAT ARE YOU DOING, THIS IS MY BIT

ELSEWHERE...
Finn? Jake? Where you guys at?

Aw, dang it.

Well, this place is a big dud! Looks like it's a lonely trip back home for ol' Ice K--
Simon?

No. It can't be.
It can't be.

Betty?

Oh my--! Simon, what happened to us?

Don't move a muscle, okay?
I trust you, sweetie.

How are you doing this?
Shhhh. Almost there.

This new hat is... EQUILATERAL!
Ruff!
Finally a dungeon prize that rules, you know?
Ruff ruff!!
Welp, time to go home!
What? Locked!
Lucky thing I've got the key RIGHT HERE!!
SWORDS AHOY, MATIES!!

ALL ABOARD THE H.M.S. SWORDS, THE BOAT MADE OUT OF, AND CAPTAINED BY, SWORDS

Aw dangs, all I've got is a flute in this world! I can't slice open sucker doors with this!
Lucky thing I've still got my LIMBS O' JUSTICE!!

Why are you growling, Jake? Are you bonkers? We have to get home--come on, help me knock this door in!
bang bang bang
GRRRRRR

GRRRRRR
CHOMP
--OUCH!

What the stuff, dude?? What's your deal??
GRRRRRR

huff huff huff
SLAM

Why do you want to leave us, Finn? You can be happy here. Everything can be perfect, like the Lich wants it to be. He hates all life, Finn. He's going to end this world soon.
He wants you to be in it when he does.
AHHHH!!

Man, Lich, why you gotta make this into a creepy time??

There's no escape, Finn. You don't need to run. You should be happy, because you don't need to do anything anymore. All you need to do is die.
AHHHHH! WHY IS EVERYTHING SO CREEPY HERE??

Okay buddy, okay, you got this. You're trapped in a creepy illusion that the Lich created, and that Jake out there is fake-o too. You need to escape this dungeon. And to do THAT, you need to do something the Lich wasn't expecting when he created this place!

What are his weaknesses? Dude was vulnerable to the GAUNTLET OF THE HERO, but that's hecka smashed. Dude was also vulnerable to THE POWER OF LIKING SOMEONE A LOT, but everyone's fake here so I can't get any love action from th--
OF COURSE!

We knew you'd come back. You have nowhere else to go, Finn. Come. This is where your story ends.
THIS GOES OUT TO THE MESSED-UP EVIL VERSION OF MY FRIEND AND ALSO TO YOU, MESSED-UP EVIL LADY!!

Ohhh the Lich is so lovely, I love him all the time / His body is so rocking, it inspires me to rhyme!
toodle doodley doooo
What are you doing?

I love him with my face and I love him with my brain / To think of a world without him makes my heart feel paaaaain!
toodle de dooodle
Why are you doing this? Stop! STOP IT!!

I love the Lich, what can I say? / I want to smooch him most of every day!!
STOP IT, THIS FRANK DISPLAY OF ALLEGED LOVE BURNS!
IT BURNS!!

No. I don't want to talk about why I wrote a comic where talking about our feelings hurts so much that it literally burns people. *MOM!!*

Hey! Hey buddy!
Jake, is it really you?!

Heh. Yeah man, it's me! I've just been chilling here with my pals!
I was trapped in a fake world and there was another you there! He chomped my arm!

Sounds nuts, bro. Anyway dude, I want you to meet, um, "Other Finn" I guess? He's actually the one with stretchy powers here! And you already know Princess Bonnibel Bubblegum.
'Sup dude.

No, Jake, you don't understand! We've got to get out of here! This whole world's gotta be an illusion too, and the Lich is behind 'em! This is his dungeon!!
Naw dude, it's fine. We destroyed the Lich part we found here. Everyone here's pretty cool!

They're not who they appear to be, Jake! They're like--fake people! Everyone here is evi--
--mmphpph!!

I'm going to chew you up, Jake. Like GUM.
Aw guys, is this SERIOUSLY like--nightmare world or something? I liked it here. You guys were chill!
YOU MADE CHILL CAKES!!

Why can't I end up in an alternate plain of existence where one single detail *ISN'T* sinisterly wrong??

Well FINE. If you're a duplicate of Finn, let's see if you're ticklish in the same spots!
Ha! S--stop! Stop, it ti--ha! It tickles!!
Whoa!

Hah! SMUSH TO SEE YOU, Peebles! And thanks for teaching me just now that good-looking peeps can be evil inside!!
It actually is a valuable life lesson. Too often we judge people by how they look and not how they act--or who they are.
DUDE OBVIOUSLY THAT'S COOL, BUT WE'RE STILL FIGHTING A STRETCHY YOU!

Right!! Let's cut him u--whoa!

Aw man!
Oh, so THAT'S what this feels like!!

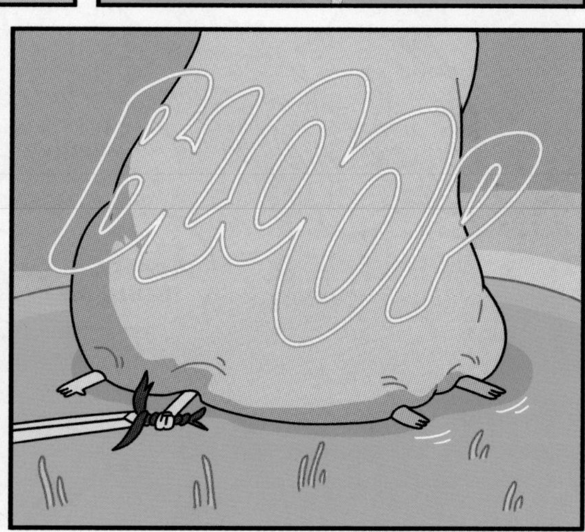

THE END. Naw. I'm just kidding. Turn the page over, there's plenty more. We have fun though, right?

Jake, these illusions are vulnerable to love ditties!
I escaped the other world by blowin' on my flute, but I don't have that here!
Aw is that all we have to do? Why didn't you say so, man?
Give me a beat!

unts unts unts chikka unts unts chik--
Yo
Yo
Yo my name is Jake, and I'm here to say / I love my friend Finn, and I hope that's okay!

whomwhoomwhooomwhoooom-whoooommmmmm BRRRRRRZZZT chicka ticka
On second thought I don't even care what you think / Because I'm not gonna stop even if you raise a stink!
AH NO I HATE HEARING ABOUT THIS!

tic toc ticca tacca pah pah pzzzztpt
We're two awesome bros, and you know it ain't a metaphor / Stop ragging on our love or I'll show you what my fists are for!
AH OTHER PEOPLE'S FEELINGS ARE SO BORING!!
ALSO THEY PHYSICALLY BURN ME!

brrm brrmmm psst bada duum-dum chk
Sorry to threaten violence but my feelings are so strong / Just don't knock our love and I know we'll get along!
LEAVE! LEAVE FOREVER!
DO NOT COME BACK. THANKS IN ADVANCE!
uh bompt brrrrpt uh bompt brrrrpt whrorrooroooo
Oh, also I love Lady Rainicorn but in a different way / Oh my glob! Don't tell her I didn't think to mention her until now, okay?
AHHHGGRHH

ATTENTION READERS: Yeah, that door was never actually locked. Nobody thought to check it! Ah well, at least we got a cool rap out of it.

Just because we don't live together doesn't mean we don't share love / Every relationship's a little bit different--kind of?
They kicked us out, dude. We don't need to rap about our feelings anymore.
Heh. **NICE.**

Where **ARE** we? This place is trashed, y'all.
Wherever it is, I can stretch again!
BUMP

I see Ice King up ahead! He's with someone! And she looks like she really wants to be there!
I wanna see!

Whoa! You're right.
Hey by the way, nice display of physical fitness, climbing up me like that!
Yay, you noticed!

Dang man, let's check it out!
Agreed!

THESIS STATEMENT: It's never not a good time for muscles! *PROOF:* My muscles. *CONCLUSION:* Hey, how much do you like my muscles??

Just a little to the left, sweetie.
Ha! Okay! It tickles when you do it.

Do you mind?
Heh. Nope.

Hey you guys! What's going on?!
You guys solving problems with your lips or what?!

Guys, you made it! I was worried about you!
Introduce me to your friends, Simon!

Oh right! This is Finn: he's like, this kid I hang out with sometimes. And this is Jake, his brother! Yeah, they're pretty okay.
Finn, Jake, I want you to meet Betty. My FIANCÉE!
Hey guys!

MAKEOUT THEATRE

THIS CONCLUDES MAKEOUT THEATRE

Dude, she's nice but this reality is totes fake! THIS is the dungeon. We need to bust out!!
We need you to help us sing emotional love raps, okay?

What? What?? You guys are crazy. Everything's real. Betty's real!
I can prove it!
Hey Bets, what's the last thing you remember?
I remember the sky being darkened by planes, and then...then the next thing I knew I was here tied up to that wall! Simon helped me get loose.

But it's fake, dude! She's fake!

No she's not. Betty, where'd we go on our first date?
Our first OFFICIAL date? Well, I suggested skating, and you went along with it even though you didn't know how. You kept falling over and over but would never admit that you just never learned how to skate.
It was sweet.

How do you know that's true? You can't remember for bums!
That's just the thing, Finn! Here I CAN remember. Here I can think clearly, see clearly. I can UNDERSTAND people!
The crown doesn't make you crazy here, it just gives you powers!
There's no cost, no price!

Show 'em, princess.
Sure!

EVERYTHING IS BEAUTIFUL AND NOTHING HURTS
See? It's fun! It's kinda like finger painting, but with your mind!
Weeee!

Everything was ice, and nothing melted.

You're not listening!! This isn't REAL. SHE'S not real. It's an illusion the Lich made!
Guys, this looks like reality, only better. This feels like reality, only better. This KISSES like reality, only way way better. If you see the Lich--

--be sure to thank him for me.

You have to come with us, dude!
Listen to me: I'M HAPPY HERE. SHE'S happy here. We can help people-- I have a castle, a queen! I'm doing good! I don't NEED to leave!
See?! We're taking care of this world. We're fine. It's a paradise here, guys. I can finally remember. I can finally BE that person I remember.
But we need to go! IT'S A TRAP!
I don't agree with you, Jake.
Come on: this isn't the dungeon! This is the PRIZE. And I'm not giving it up!

I'm sorry, Ice King. I wish there was another way.
Yeah, well, I'm sorry too. I really am. But I'm staying, so, see you later or whatever.

Alright. Ready, Finn?
Ready Jake. Hold on tight.
These beats will be DANGEROUSLY fresh.

brrm brrrrm brrrroooooooooomm chicka
wikki wikki

These beats are dangerously fresh: they're not on *ANY* hooks! They're outside the range of our sight! They're taking some envelopes and pushing them around!

Ow!
Huh?
Yo, Jake's on the mic and your breath is bated!
He's gonna get some feels out, get y'all elated!

Ice King, our status: complicated but we're doing what we do 'cause you're loved not hated!
And though this woman you think you dated, you know she's not the one you've that long awaited!
It's--ah! It hurting me, Simon! Make them stop!
Finn, Jake! Stop it!!

Can't you see you're hurting her?!
Betty's not real: she's Lich-related, Betty's memory desecrated! It's not something that I'll see debated: this illusionary world must be negated!!
Ahhh! AHHHHHH!

Simon, I--I don't feel fake--
You're not sweetie, you're not, you're not. I love you. You know that.
You're just as real as I--

KAPOW

--as I remember.

I'm sorry! I'm sorry! But it had to be done. It was--
--it was the only way home.

Let's get the butt out of here.

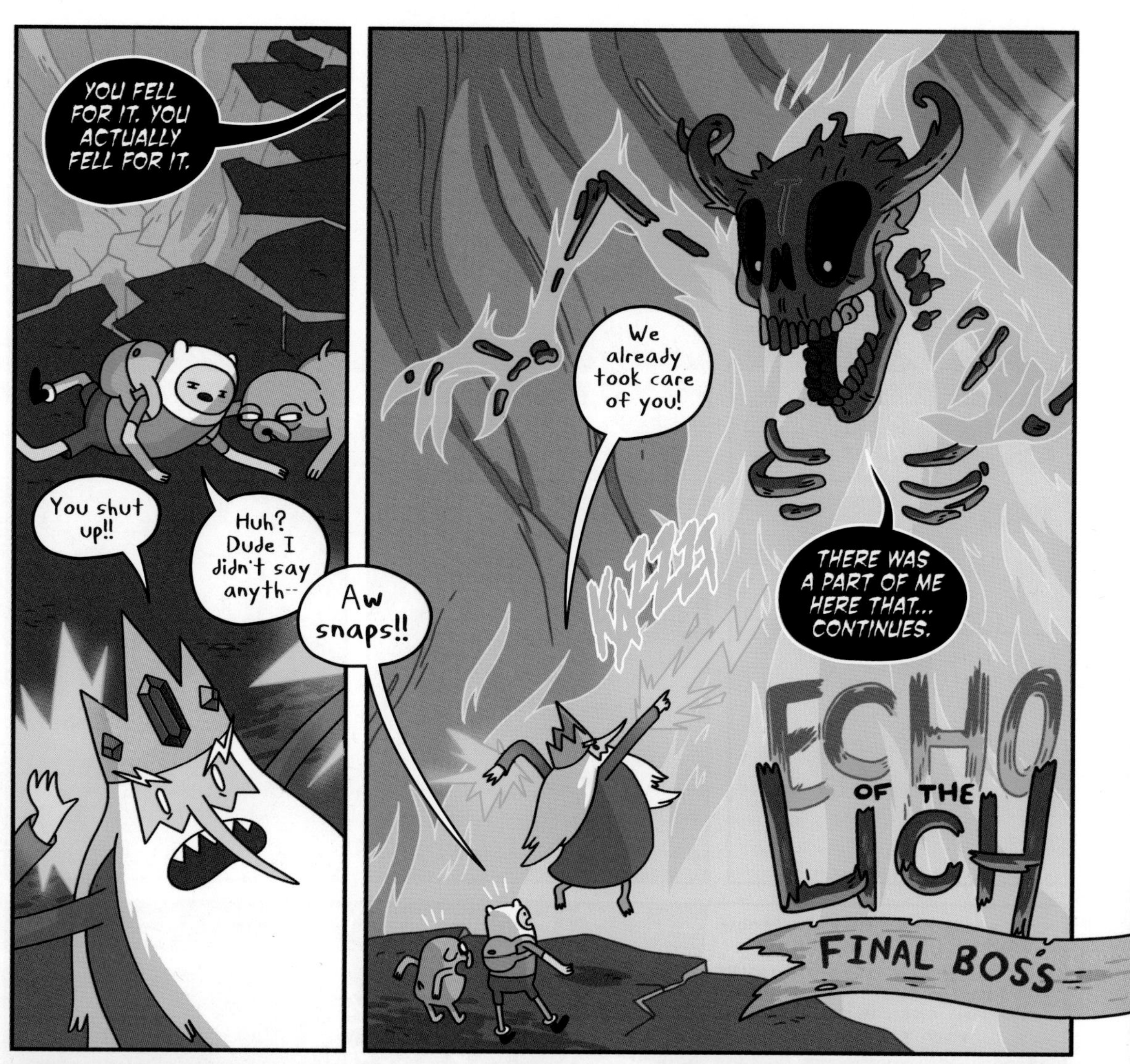
YOU FELL FOR IT. YOU ACTUALLY FELL FOR IT.
You shut up!!
Huh? Dude I didn't say anyth--
Aw snaps!!
We already took care of you!
KAZZZT
THERE WAS A PART OF ME HERE THAT... CONTINUES.
ECHO OF THE LICH
FINAL BOSS

Why?! Why create a dungeon just to mess with our heads?!
KAZZZT
SWORD ATTACK COMBO!
I AM THE SECOND SWORD!!
IT WAS SO EASY TO TRICK YOU. YOU WANTED IT SO BADLY TO BE REAL.

ONCE I WAS INSIDE YOUR HEAD, I KNEW YOUR SECRETS. I KNEW YOUR FAILURES.
I KNEW THE PEOPLE YOU'VE HURT, AND BETTER, THE PEOPLE YOU'VE LET BE HURT.
Ow!
Gah!

Man remember a few pages ago when everything was easy and fun and we even got to have a makeout theatre down here? Good times, good times!

WHY DO YOU FIGHT?
IT'S HOPELESS. YOU'RE A JOKE, AN OLD MAN WHO CAN'T EVEN REMEMBER HIS NAME.
It's true. I forget important things sometimes...

Sometimes I do think I should give up--just let the crown win and the world freeze, with me in it.
Some days I can't remember a single reason to keep fighting.

Some...some days I--I can't even remember her.
YOU'RE A LOSER. NOBODY LIKES YOU. NOBODY EVEN WANTS TO LIKE YOU.

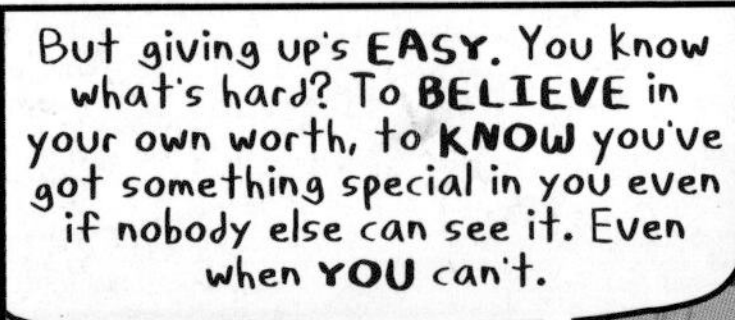
But giving up's EASY. You know what's hard? To BELIEVE in your own worth, to KNOW you've got something special in you even if nobody else can see it. Even when YOU can't.

YOU DON'T HAVE ANYTHING SPECIAL IN YOU. YOU'RE GOING TO BE ALONE FOREVER.
YOU'RE GOING TO DIE ALONE. ALL ALONE.

Yeah, maybe.

But at least that means I'm not dying today, you CHUMP!!

NO! YOU CAN'T--
KA-
CRACK
Just did, bucko.

Dude, I keep getting body junk dumped on me in this adventure.
Roll with it, buddy!

PING
Treasure? After all that?
Whoa, Jake! Are you saying that maybe the true treasure is FRIENDSHIP? COMPANIONSHIP? ULTIMATE BROTIMES??

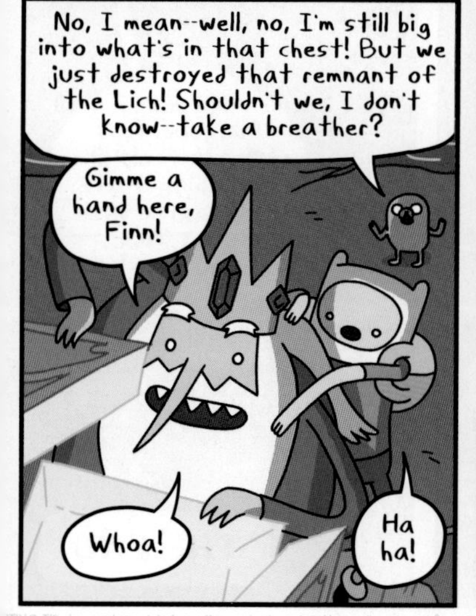
No, I mean--well, no, I'm still big into what's in that chest! But we just destroyed that remnant of the Lich! Shouldn't we, I don't know--take a breather?
Gimme a hand here, Finn!
Whoa!
Ha ha!

I mean, is it REALLY appropriate to celebrate right now by opening up some old chest and taking--

--AN ACTUAL REAL-LIFE MAILMAN'S OUTFIT?!
AHHHH! I LOVE IT!

ITING TIP: to capture Jake's excitement at seeing the mailman's outfit, I just imagine how I feel whenever I see an actual real-life astronaut's outfit. AHHH SPACE IS SO AWESOME, I WANNA GO THERE PLEASE!

And I got **A NEW SWORD!**
AHHH IT'S SO GREAT!

A perfect fit.

You guys ready to go?
Yeah mans!
Neither snow nor rain nor heat nor gloom of night stays me from the swift completion of my appointed rounds!!

Hey, does anyone else have a bit of a tummy-ache?
Nope! Is this a problem I can solve with swords??

No man, I'm good. But **WOW** it feels like something I ate didn't agree with me **AT ALL**, you guys!
Bleh!
THE END.

AFTER-CREDITS SCENE: Finn and Jake rap about how much they like the Lich, just to make sure they ARE actually in reality now. BMO is confused and saddened to hear this rap and refuses to join in, even on the "can I get what what" parts. He straight-up refuses to give them a what what.

COVER GALLERY

Cover 15A:
Mike Holmes
MIKE
HOLMES.

EMILY
WARREN
Cover 15B:
Emily Warren

Cover 15C:
Nidhi Chanani

Nidhi
Chanani

Cover 15D:
Spike Trautman

kaboom!
MARCELINE
the Vampire Queen
TM
15
APR
jjwharrison
Brett's Collector's Edition:
JJ Harrison

Awesome Con Exclusive:
Mark Mariano

TESSA STONE! '13

C2E2 Exclusive:
Tessa Stone

Calgary Expo Exclusive:
Shoichi Uehara

Cover 16A:
Mike Holmes

MIKE HOLMES.
PROPS TO P.F.T.!

jjwharrison

Cover 16B:
JJ Harrison

Cover 16C:
Sophie Goldstein
Sophie
Goldstein

m.mcclaren
Cover 16D:
Meredith McClaren

Bleeding Cool Awards Exclusive:
Kris Mukai
HUG
BMO

Hot Topic Exclusive:
Meredith McClaren
m.mcclaren

SuperCon Exclusive:
Mad Rupert
ADVENTURE TIME™
featuring:
"THE LEGION OF AWESOME FRIENDS"
finn
Jake
LEGUM
YES
NO
YES
NO
EXTRA: ICE KING CONFIRMED FOR TOTAL BUTTHEAD
KaBOOM!

Cover 17A:
Chris Houghton
Colors: Kassandra Heller
:D
BMO
CHRIS HOUGHTON

Cover 17B:
Erika Moen

BMO
Erika Moen '13

Cover 17C:
Jemma Salume

M. MCCLAREN
Cover 17D:
Meredith McClaren

Mondo Exclusive:
JJ Harrison
jjwharrison

SP/BL

Boston Comic Con Exclusive:
Shelli Paroline & Braden Lamb

Cover 18A:
Mike Holmes
BMO
MIKE
HOLMES.

Cover 18B:
Kelly Bastow

Cover 18C:
Caroline Breault

Cover 18D:
Yehudi Mercado
Niño Macho
El Perro Elástico
Princesa de Chicle
TIEMPO de
AVENTURA
YEHUDI MERCADO

San Diego Comic-Con Exclusive:
Bryan Turner

Newbury Comics Exclusive:
Maris Wicks

CBLDF Exclusive:
Chrystin Garland

Cover 19A:
Mike Holmes

Cover 19B:
Britt Sanders

Cover 19C:
Matt Sheean

Cover 19D:
Chris Visions